This book belongs

To: <u>Angelina Marie Benavides</u>

<u>if lost (831) 637-4371</u>

HORSE SENSE

BOOK SERIES

Published By

OHC Group LLC
PO Box 7839, Westlake Village, CA 91359

SECOND EDITION
ISBN 0-9763213-2-7

Printed and bound in China

The Only Hearts Girls™ formed
The Only Hearts Club® in a bond
of true friendship. They are a fun-
loving bunch of friends who are
always there for one another. They
laugh, share secrets and have the
greatest adventures together. Most
importantly, they encourage one
another to listen to their hearts
and do the right thing.

Contents

Olivia Has Big News

Olivia Hope and her yellow Labrador retriever, Sniff, hurried down the street. They were headed to Olivia's favorite ice cream shop, Swirls, to meet up with her friends from the Only Hearts Club, a fun-loving group of six girls who were always there for one another. They laughed, shared secrets and had the greatest adventures together. Most importantly, they thought with their hearts and always tried to do the right thing – even though it wasn't always easy to do. As Olivia walked, her chestnut brown hair danced behind her in the breeze, and her blue eyes sparkled with anticipation.

When she turned the corner, she saw her friends waiting for her at a table outside Swirls. They were all there with their dogs. Taylor Angelique and her beagle, Patches; Karina Grace and her dalmatian, Dotcom; Briana Joy and her dachshund, Longfellow; Lily Rose and her terrier, Cupcake; and Anna Sophia and her cocker spaniel, Bubulina.

"Hi!" Olivia called. Sniff barked, happy to see that all his buddies were there.

"Hi, Olivia!" Taylor called back. "Happy almost birthday!"

The girls giggled and Olivia grinned. Tomorrow was her birthday, and Olivia's parents were hosting a party in the afternoon for all her friends. She could hardly wait!

"Let's get ice cream cones," said Anna, who was happiest making or eating food.

As they waited in line for their cones, Briana asked, "What do you want for your birthday, Olivia?"

Olivia hesitated. *Should I tell them my secret?* she wondered.

"What's that look in your eyes?" Lily asked Olivia.

"Oh…nothing," Olivia said, not too convincingly. All the girls stopped and looked at her with smiles on their faces.

"Olivia's got a secret, Olivia's got a secret," Karina Grace chanted in her lovely voice while leaning her head backward so that her long, pretty blond hair fell behind her.

"Come on, Olivia," Anna urged, her brown eyes shining. "Spill the beans."

Olivia didn't need much prodding to share her "secret."

"Well," she began, "you know how much I like horses?"

"*Like* them?" Taylor laughed. "Olivia, you totally *love horses* and horseback riding!"

"You spend so much time at the stables that I heard they were going to give you your own stall so you could spend the night!" Lily teased as she twirled a strand of strawberry blond hair around her finger. All the girls laughed, including Olivia.

Olivia's friends were right. She absolutely adored horses. Every week she had a riding lesson at Windy Way Stables. It was fun to groom and ride Duke, the gentle Appaloosa. The only problem with Windy Way Stables was that Olivia couldn't just go there and ride Duke whenever she wanted to. She had to wait for her lesson each week.

"Well, you all know that having my own horse is my

dream," Olivia continued.

"Yes! Yes!" they all answered, drawing close to Olivia in anticipation of what she was going to say next.

"Well...I'm getting one!" Olivia blurted out before covering her mouth with her hands.

The Only Hearts Club girls let out a collective scream of excitement and delight.

"That's totally awesome!" Briana shouted as she jumped up and down with her curly brown hair flying around her head. "I'm so happy for you!"

"Are you sure?" Taylor asked Olivia. "How do you know?"

"Well, I saw a note my mother left by the phone," Olivia confided. "It said 'Call Ms. Anderson about the horse.'"

"Ms. Anderson your riding teacher?" Karina asked.

Olivia nodded. "If Mom was calling her about a horse, it must be because she's buying me one for my birthday! I mean, I've been asking my parents for a horse for as long as I can remember."

"Are you sure that's what the note meant?" Taylor asked, sounding a bit skeptical.

Lily raised her eyebrows and shot Taylor a look that said, "Hey, cut it out!"

"I mean, I'm just asking," shrugged Taylor, her wavy dark blond hair framing her pretty face.

Olivia frowned and thought. The note didn't exactly say "Call Ms. Anderson to buy a horse." *Why was Taylor being such a party pooper?* Olivia wondered. Well, she wasn't going to let it ruin her exciting news. She turned and said, "Yes, Taylor, I'm sure that's what it meant."

"It's just...well, horses are so expensive," Briana added.

Olivia scowled. Sure, horses were expensive, and Olivia's parents certainly weren't rich. But she thought her friends were starting to sound jealous.

"Look, guys, I'm getting a horse for my birthday, OK?" Olivia insisted. She knew she was trying to convince herself as much as her friends. "If you don't believe me, just wait; you'll see!"

"Oh, Olivia, you're so lucky!" Karina cried.

"I can't wait to meet your new horse," Briana said.

"When I get my horse, I'll take you all for rides," Olivia promised.

"Ooh, thank you!" the girls exclaimed. Even Taylor appeared impressed.

Olivia looked at the ice cream in the display case. She could almost taste the sweet chocolate in her mouth. But hearing her friends so impressed and excited was an even sweeter sensation. And when they saw her riding her own horse and proving Taylor wrong – well, that would be an ice cream sundae with a cherry on top!

The Birthday Present

The next morning, Olivia woke up and let out a big yawn. Her heart soared when she remembered what day it was. "It's my birthday, Sniff!" she cried, reaching down to pet him as he slept peacefully in his dog bed at the foot of her bed. "I can't wait for my present!"

She leaped out of bed, swept her long dark hair into a pony tail and ran to the kitchen. Her parents were sitting at the table, drinking coffee. Melanie, her older sister, was pouring orange juice.

"Happy birthday, Olivia!" they all exclaimed together.

"I'm making your favorite blueberry pancakes," her mother said.

"Then we can give you your present," her father added.

It was hard for Olivia to concentrate on food right now. All she could think about was her horse. She had begged and begged her parents for one, and now her dream was about to come true!

What would it be? she wondered. *Maybe it's Duke,* she thought. *Or maybe it's a mustang or an Arabian.* Whatever it was, she knew she would love it forever.

Finally, breakfast ended and Olivia's father went to get her present. When he came back, he was holding an envelope. Eagerly, Olivia ripped it open. Inside was a photograph of a beautiful golden brown horse. Olivia's heart almost leaped out of her chest! "That's Missy!" she cried. "I've seen her at Windy Way Stables. Oh, Mom and Dad, I had a feeling this was the year you were going to buy me the horse I've always wanted! Thank you! Thank you! Thank you!"

Her mother and father just looked at each other. Her father started to speak, but before he could say anything, Olivia asked a question. "Who's this?" she said, looking at the picture. Standing beside the horse in the photograph was her teacher, Ms. Anderson, and a woman with gray hair whom Olivia had never seen before.

"That's Missy's owner, Mrs. Brooks," her mother explained.

"So that's who you bought Missy from?" Olivia asked with a smile. "What did she tell you about Missy? When can I go see my new horse?"

Her parents paused and looked at each other again. "Olivia, honey, we can't afford to buy you a horse," her father said gently, "so we leased one instead. We leased Missy for you to ride."

"Leased? What does that mean? She's still my horse, right?" Olivia asked uncertainly.

"It's a bit like renting," her mother answered. "Missy belongs to Mrs. Brooks, but you can ride her for your lessons twice a week."

Olivia's heart sank. She knew she should be happy. Her parents had done the best they could to please her. But deep inside, she was so disappointed she wanted to cry.

Missy isn't mine, she thought sadly to herself. *She's just a rent-a-horse.*

"Thanks, Mom and Dad," she said, forcing herself to smile – a smile that was a lot smaller than the one she'd had when she first opened the envelope.

The Birthday Party

Olivia sat on her bed, biting her nails. Soon her friends would arrive for her birthday party. Normally, she would be all smiles, but now everything was different. Her friends were expecting her to tell them about her new horse.

Why did I open my big mouth? she wondered. She wished she had never told her friends she was getting a horse. It turned out that Olivia had been wrong to assume her parents were buying her a horse, and her friends were right when they questioned her about it. Ooh! She didn't want to hear them say "I told you so!"

Just then the doorbell rang. "Olivia, your friends are here," her mother called.

With her stomach churning, Olivia went to the front door to meet them.

"Happy birthday!" they shouted as they piled through the door.

"Where's your present?" Taylor asked, pretending to look around the room for a horse.

"Is it in the backyard?" Karina teased.

"Not exactly," Olivia said. "Come to my room and I'll tell you."

As bad as it made her feel, Olivia was going to tell them the truth. But when they got to her room and she saw their eager, expectant eyes, she hesitated. How could she tell them the truth? She had told them that she was sure her parents were buying her a horse. She had even promised them all rides on her new horse. But she couldn't give rides on a horse that wasn't hers.

"So, where's your horse?" Briana asked with a smile.

"When can we see it?" Anna chimed in.

"And ride it?" Lily begged.

Olivia looked at her shoes. She had to be honest with her friends. But it was so hard!

When she looked up, Taylor was gazing at her curiously. "You didn't get one, did you?" she said. Taylor sounded so sure of herself that Olivia couldn't stand it.

"I did, too!" she blurted out. "Look at this if you

don't believe me."

She grabbed the photo of Missy from her desk and handed it to Taylor. The girls leaned in to look.

"What a pretty horse!" Karina cried.

"What's his name?" asked Lily.

"It's a mare and her name is Missy," Olivia said.

"Who are those people?" Taylor asked, pointing to Ms. Anderson and Mrs. Brooks.

"That's my riding teacher," Olivia said. "And that lady…uh, she's the person who sold Missy to my parents."

Taylor smiled. "I'm glad I was wrong," she said. "She's beautiful and you deserve her."

Finally Olivia had quieted know-it-all Taylor. *Besides,* she thought, *no one needs to know who really owns the horse, just that it's mine to ride.*

The following day was Olivia's riding lesson at Windy Way Stables.

"I think you're going to like Missy," Ms. Anderson said. "She's got a lot of spunk – not like pokey old Duke."

Olivia brought Missy out of her stable and tied her to the hitching post. She was a beautiful horse – strong and sleek with big, brown eyes and a long, thick mane. Ms. Anderson was right about her spirit. As Olivia put the saddle on, Missy pawed the ground, eager to get into the ring.

Olivia climbed on. "Here we go, girl," she said, stroking Missy's neck.

Ms. Anderson set up some orange cones and asked Olivia to lead Missy in some figure eights. First they walked, then they trotted.

"She's fabulous!" Olivia cried as they rounded the cones.

"Would you like to try a canter?" her teacher asked. "All you have to do is lean forward and ask her."

Olivia leaned forward. "Let's go, girl!"

Instantly, Missy broke into an easy canter. Olivia led the graceful mare through a series of figure eights.

I only have to think a command and Missy follows it, Olivia thought happily. *It's as if we've been together forever. As if Missy were mine...*

Just then, Missy veered to the edge of the ring and stopped so fast that Olivia almost fell off.

"Oh, my goodness! I'm sorry, Olivia," a voice exclaimed.

Olivia looked up to see Mrs. Brooks standing there. "I didn't mean to cause trouble. I just wanted to introduce myself. I'm Mrs. Brooks, Missy's owner."

Olivia's heart sank again. While she was riding, she had pretended that Missy was hers. *How silly,* she thought now.

"Hello, Mrs. Brooks," she said, trying hard to smile and hide her disappointment.

Mrs. Brooks smiled. "You look very nice up there, Olivia. Have you thought about competing in the Long Grove Horse Show in a few weeks?"

"No. I don't have a horse to ride," Olivia answered. "Duke's too old."

"You can use Missy if you want," Mrs. Brooks said kindly.

"Do you mean it?" Olivia exclaimed. "Oh, thank you!"

Olivia couldn't believe it! She was going to compete in a horse show – her very first horse show – with the smartest, most perfect horse in the world!

Covering Up the Truth

Look at all the pretty horses!" Taylor exclaimed as she, Lily and Olivia climbed out of the minivan to visit Windy Way Stables a few days later.

"How many horses live here, Olivia?" Lily asked.

"At least twenty-five," Olivia replied. "Come on, I'll show you Missy."

Olivia smiled as they walked to the barn. The girls had been asking to see Missy all week.

"I'll be back in an hour to pick you up," Olivia's mother called as she drove away.

Olivia threw open the barn door and led the girls inside. "There she is."

"She's gorgeous!" Taylor cried.

"You're so lucky to own your own horse," Lily said.

Olivia looked around. Had anyone from the stables heard that?

"Let's brush her," Olivia said. She brought Missy to the hitching post, then got the brushes and gave one to each girl.

"Can we ride her?" Taylor asked.

Olivia didn't know what to say. Only she was permitted to ride Missy. "Maybe," she lied again – she was getting in deeper – "if you do a good job brushing her."

Taylor frowned and Olivia looked away. She knew she sounded bossy, but what could she do? She gave each girl a carrot to feed to Missy.

When Missy swallowed the last one, Lily asked, "Now can we ride her?"

Olivia thought fast, wanting to say the truth, but not knowing how. Just then, Ms. Anderson walked by the stable door with an animal.

"What's that?" Taylor asked.

"A miniature horse," Olivia replied. "His name is Buster."

"Can we pet him?" Lily asked.

"Sure. Go ahead." Olivia relaxed as the girls ran out the door to find Buster. Alone in the barn, Olivia put her arms around Missy's neck. "I love you, Missy," she whispered in her ear. "I wish you were mine."

Suddenly, Olivia heard a noise at the door. She looked up, expecting to see Taylor and Lily, but it was Mrs. Brooks.

Olivia froze. She didn't want to talk to Mrs. Brooks now. And what if Taylor and Lily came back while Mrs. Brooks was there? She might say something about being Missy's owner. Then the girls would know the truth, and Olivia would never live it down.

Olivia stepped behind Missy and looked around frantically for a place to hide. Then she had a better idea. There was a dark green garden hose in the corner, which was used to fill the horses' water troughs. She grabbed it and wiggled it around on the ground.

"A snake!" Olivia screamed. "There's a snake in the barn!"

Mrs. Brooks screamed. "Oh, dear, don't get too close! I'll go and get help."

Mrs. Brooks ran out of the barn. Olivia put the hose down and wondered what to do next. Just then, Taylor and Lily appeared at the barn door. "We heard a scream," Taylor said. "What's going on?"

"Uh…I saw a snake," Olivia said.

"A snake!" Taylor cried. "Let's get out of here!"

The girls ran out of the barn door just as Mrs. Brooks and Ms. Anderson ran in the other side. "Where's the snake?" Ms. Anderson asked. "Did you see it, Olivia?"

"It was in Missy's stall," she lied.

"OK," Ms. Anderson said. "You go outside. I'll take care of this."

Olivia didn't have to be told twice. She ran outside and joined her friends. "We'd better not go back in the barn today."

"Oh, no!" Taylor gasped. "What if it bites Missy?"

Olivia pretended to look worried. But inside, she was relieved. Now her only worry was what would happen if Mrs. Brooks came out of the barn while she was still there.

"Oh, look, here comes your mom," Lily said.

Olivia had never been so happy to see her mother's minivan. Eagerly, she ran to meet it.

See You Soon, Duke

Olivia practiced with Missy for two straight weeks. When she passed Duke's stall, he looked at her sadly.

"Don't worry, boy, we'll be riding together again soon," she said quietly. Duke seemed to be the only one she told the truth to lately. Olivia had never come so close to having a dream come true – yet she was miserable. She had told her friends so many fibs about the horse that now she was trying to avoid them so she wouldn't have to answer any more questions. That made her more miserable, but she couldn't stand lying to them anymore. Eventually, she'd have to go back to riding Duke, and then she'd make up one last lie about Missy being too big for her or having to go live someplace else. Then it would all be over and she could have her life back. For now, at least she could enjoy riding this magnificent horse.

The Horse Show

On the morning of the Long Grove Horse Show, Olivia was so excited she could hardly stand it. She stood by the horse trailer, brushing the beautiful golden brown horse. "Good girl, Missy," she said. "I just know we're going to do well today."

"Attention, please," said the voice over the loud speaker. "Contestants in the 'Twelve and Under' category, please report to Gate Three."

"That's you," Ms. Anderson said with an encouraging smile. "Good luck, Olivia."

Olivia's heart was pounding as she straddled Missy and walked her to Gate 3. A few of the contestants were already there. They were wearing brand-new navy blue jackets, spotless tan breeches, and shiny black leather boots.

Olivia sighed. Aside from the breeches her grandparents had given her for her birthday, her riding clothes were far from new. Still, her boots were polished and shiny, and her jacket and breeches were clean and neatly pressed.

It isn't new clothes that win the competition, she reminded herself. *It's the one who rides the best.* She reached down to pat Missy's neck.

"Let's show them what we can do, girl," she said to her horse. Missy responded by lifting her head proudly. As they approached the gate to the ring, Olivia suddenly lurched forward in the saddle as Missy stumbled on a hidden rock.

Missy stopped in her tracks.

"What's wrong, Missy?" Olivia asked.

Missy took a step, but seemed to hesitate. Olivia looked down. The mare was holding her left front hoof slightly off the ground.

Olivia bit her lip. Maybe she should go back to the trailer and tell Ms. Anderson, she thought. But there was no time. If Olivia wasn't there when the competition started, she'd be disqualified. But Missy seemed to be hurt, and riding her could make it worse.

Olivia looked through the gate and spotted her

parents and her sister sitting in the stands. How eager and excited they looked! She didn't want to let them down. Then she noticed Mrs. Brooks sitting right behind them. She didn't want to let her down either – not after she'd been so kind to let Olivia ride Missy today.

"Olivia, over here!" a voice called.

Olivia looked up to see her friends from the Only Hearts Club walking toward her.

"We came to wish you luck," Karina said.

"We just know you're going to shine today," Briana added.

If Olivia had been confused before, she was positively paralyzed now. How could she tell Mrs. Brooks that her horse was lame while the girls were there? They'd find out Missy didn't really belong to her.

The loud speaker crackled. "Contestants in the 'Twelve and Under' category, please enter the ring," the announcer said.

"Good luck," Olivia's friends called out together as they left her at the gate and ran to take seats in the stands.

Olivia was in a panic. Her parents and friends

were all there to see her ride her new horse and win a blue ribbon in the horse show. *I have to ride in this competition, don't I? she thought to herself. She's not even my horse. Maybe I should just go ahead and ride her and hope it doesn't hurt her even more.*

To buy time, she walked Missy in a small circle outside the gate. There was no doubt about it – the mare was limping. It wasn't much of a limp, just a slight hesitation that someone watching from the stands wouldn't see. But Olivia was on the horse, and she could tell.

Olivia's heart was heavy, but she knew what that feeling meant. After all, she was a member of the Only Hearts Club. She and her friends had promised to listen to their hearts and do the right thing. She knew that's what she had to do right now. Missy was hurt, and if Olivia rode her in the competition, she might be hurt more seriously. She had to see a veterinarian right away! Making sure Missy was OK was more important than trying to impress her friends. It was the right thing to do.

Olivia leaned down and hugged Missy's neck. Oh,

how she loved this perfect horse! She never wanted her to be in pain. Never! She had to tell Mrs. Brooks about Missy's injury.

Olivia Listens to Her Heart

With her heart fluttering, Olivia walked Missy into the ring. But instead of walking her around the arena with the other riders, she led her slowly to the edge of the fence near the stands. Then she caught Mrs. Brooks's eye.

Mrs. Brooks jumped to her feet and hurried down to the fence. "What is it, Olivia?"

Quickly, Olivia explained what was wrong.

"Oh, my!" Mrs. Brooks exclaimed. "Please stay right here, and don't let Missy move! I'll go find the vet."

Olivia climbed off Missy. Soon her friends were standing across the railing from her. "What's wrong?" Taylor asked. "Who was that woman you were talking to?"

Olivia hesitated. Maybe she could still convince her friends that Missy was hers. But it was too confusing to keep covering up the truth. Besides, she knew in her heart it wasn't right.

"That was Missy's owner, Mrs. Brooks," Olivia admitted solemnly.

"What?" Karina exclaimed. "I thought Missy was yours."

"That's what I wanted you to think. Actually, my parents couldn't afford to buy me a horse, so they leased Missy. I can ride her twice a week for a year, but that's all. She's not mine."

Olivia hung her head and waited for the girls to say "I told you so," especially Taylor. But instead, they reached across the railing and hugged her.

"You wanted your own horse so badly," Briana said. "You must have been so disappointed."

"But why did you pull out of the competition?" Lily asked.

"Missy's limping," Olivia answered. "She hurt her hoof on a rock. Riding today might have hurt her even more. So I decided to tell Mrs. Brooks and keep Missy out of the competition."

Taylor's eyes met Olivia's and Olivia was sure she was about to say that she knew Olivia hadn't gotten a

horse for her birthday. Instead, Taylor said, "That was really thoughtful of you, Olivia. I bet Mrs. Brooks is grateful, and I'm sure Missy *really* appreciates what you just did."

Olivia felt her heart overflow. She *had* done the right thing! "I'm grateful too," Olivia said, "for friends like you. I'm sorry about this whole horse thing. I just wanted one so badly that I made myself believe it was going to happen. Then I started making up stories to you because I was embarrassed about the truth. I really let it get out of hand. I'm sorry."

"Olivia," Taylor said, reaching through the fence to put her hand on her friend's shoulder. "We'll all be best friends whether you have a horse or not. We don't care whether your horse is leased or whatever. We just want you to be happy. The important thing is that you listened to your heart and did the right thing."

Missy Says, "Thanks"

A few minutes later, Mrs. Brooks arrived with the veterinarian, who looked at Missy's hoof and asked Olivia to walk her back to the trailer slowly. She led the mare along, with the Only Hearts Girls by her side. When they arrived at the trailer, the vet examined the bottom of Missy's hoof more carefully.

"Luckily it's just a deep cut, nothing more," he said. "She'll be fine, but she'll have to take it easy for a while."

Olivia sighed with relief.

"But a cut like that can get infected quickly," the vet said. "And though it's not serious, it could have been had she been ridden in the show today. Whoever decided not to ride her and to call me made a smart move!" The vet told Mrs. Brooks how to care for Missy's cut. Then he closed his medical kit and tipped his cowboy hat. "Good day, ladies."

Mrs. Brooks turned to Olivia. "Thank you, Olivia,"

she said. "You really did the right thing. You took care of Missy, even thought it meant dropping out of the competition."

Olivia smiled proudly. Then she hugged Missy and buried her face in the pretty horse's neck. "I love you, Missy," she whispered. Missy nuzzled Olivia, almost as if she knew Olivia had helped her.

Good News for Everyone

That afternoon, ribbons were given out to the winners of the horse show. Olivia sat in the stands with her family and all her friends.

"And now, the winner of the 'Twelve and Under' competition," the announcer said. "Molly Connors."

A girl in a navy riding jacket rode her horse into the ring to accept her blue ribbon. Olivia applauded, even though deep in her heart she couldn't help wishing it had been her.

Everyone cheered for Molly, then prepared to head home. But Olivia wasn't ready to leave just yet.

"I'll be right back," she told her friends.

With her long brown hair streaming behind her, she ran to Mrs. Brooks's horse trailer. Missy was lying nearby, munching some hay. When Missy saw Olivia, she lifted her head and whinnied happily.

"I just wanted to check on you one more time

42

before I left," Olivia said softly to Missy, patting her gently on the nose.

"You're turning into quite a horsewoman," a voice said. Olivia spun around. Mrs. Brooks was standing there with a big smile on her face. Behind her were Olivia's friends. "I can see that not only are you a splendid rider, but you're also a caring young lady." Mrs. Brooks sat back on her heels and narrowed her eyes as if thinking about something. Then she spoke again. "Olivia," she said, "how would you like to ride Missy on Saturdays and Sundays – for free?"

"Really?!" Olivia cried. She was so happy! Now she could ride Missy four days a week if she wanted to!

"And you can bring a friend to ride her each time, too," added Mrs. Brooks. The girls shrieked with glee.

Olivia turned to Missy and crouched down. "Did you hear that, girl? As soon as your cut is healed, I'm going to take you on a nice, long ride!" Missy bobbed her head, then rested her chin on Olivia's shoulder.

Taylor smiled at her friend and said, "Good things really do happen when you listen to your heart and do the right thing!"

Read all the Only Hearts Girls' heartwarming storybooks.

It's Hard To Say Good-Bye
When her friend loses her dog, Taylor Angelique finds a new puppy for her. But will Taylor Angelique keep the cute little puppy for herself?

Horse Sense
Olivia Hope's horse develops a slight limp right before the big show. Will she go for the blue ribbon or choose to save her horse?

Dancing Dilemma
Karina Grace is the best dancer in school. Will she let her talent get in the way of her friendships?

Teamwork Works
Briana Joy is a superstar on the soccer field. Will she try to win the game by herself or be a good teammate and help a friend?

Two Smart Cookies
Anna Sophia's pie is ruined just hours before the big bake-off. Can she whip up Grandma's secret recipe in time?

Peep for Keeps
Lily Rose discovers a lost baby bird in the forest. Should she keep it as a pet or return it to nature?